Sticker Activity Book

PETER RABBIT™
& Friends

From the original and authorized stories by

BEATRIX POTTER™

F. WARNE & CO

How to use this book

To use the stickers in this book, open out the folded scene on either the front or the back inside cover and lay it flat. Carefully remove the sticker section from the center of the book and peel the individual stickers off and stick them on to the background you have chosen to create your own scene. When you have finished, peel the stickers off again and replace them on the backing sheet they came from ready to use again. You will then be able to use and reuse the stickers as many times as you like.

FREDERICK WARNE

Published by the Penguin Group
Penguin Books Ltd, 27 Wrights Lane, London W8 5TZ, England
Penguin Putnam Inc., 375 Hudson Street, New York, N.Y. 10014, USA
Penguin Books Australia Ltd, Ringwood, Victoria, Australia
Penguin Books Canada Ltd, 10 Alcorn Avenue, Toronto, Ontario, Canada M4V 3B2
Penguin Books NZ Ltd, Private Bag 102902, NSMC, Aukland, New Zealand
Penguin Books India (P) Ltd, 11 Community Centre, Panchsheel Park, New Delhi, 110 017, India
Penguin Books (South Africa) (Pty) Ltd, 5 Watkins Street, Denver Ext 4, 2094, South Africa

Penguin Books Ltd, Registered Offices: Harmondsworth, Middlesex, England
Visit our web site at: www.peterrabbit.com
First published by Frederick Warne 2000
1 2 3 4 5 6 7 8 9 10
Copyright © Frederick Warne & Co., 2000
Beatrix Potter's illustrations copyright © Frederick Warne & Co., 1904
Illustrations from The World of Peter Rabbit and Friends™ animated television and video series, a TV Cartoons Ltd production
for Frederick Warne & Co., copyright © Frederick Warne & Co., 1992, 1993, 1994, 1995, 1996

ISBN 0 7232 4681 5

Printed and bound in Italy by Imago

Additional illustrations by Colin Twinn and Rowan Clifford

Character Links

Here are some favorite Beatrix Potter characters. Draw a line between each character and the item that is linked to them.

Connect the Dot

Join the dots to reveal who is having their face washed ready for a tea party.
When you have finished, color the picture in.

Squirrel Nutkin's Riddles

Can you guess the answers to these riddles. Use the clues to help you.

Ninny Nanny Netticoat

Ninny Nanny Netticoat,
In a white petticoat,
*   With a red nose -*
The longer she stands,
The shorter she grows.

Clue: it is made of wax

Hitty Pitty

Hitty Pitty within the wall,
Hitty Pitty without the wall;
If you touch Hitty Pitty,
Hitty Pitty will bite you!

Clue: a plant that stings

Riddle me, Riddle me, Rot-tot-tote!

Riddle me, riddle me, rot-tot-tote!
A little wee man, in a red red coat!
A staff in his hand, and a stone in his throat;
If you'll tell me this riddle, I'll give you a groat.

Clue: a fruit that can be made into jam

Chimney Maze

Here is a three part maze, which shows what happened to Tom Kitten when he climbed up the chimney and met two rats, Samuel Whiskers and Anna Maria. First, trace the path Tom took to reach the rats' room. Then, see how the carpenter dog, John Joiner, tunneled down to rescue him. Finally, find out how the rats themselves escaped.

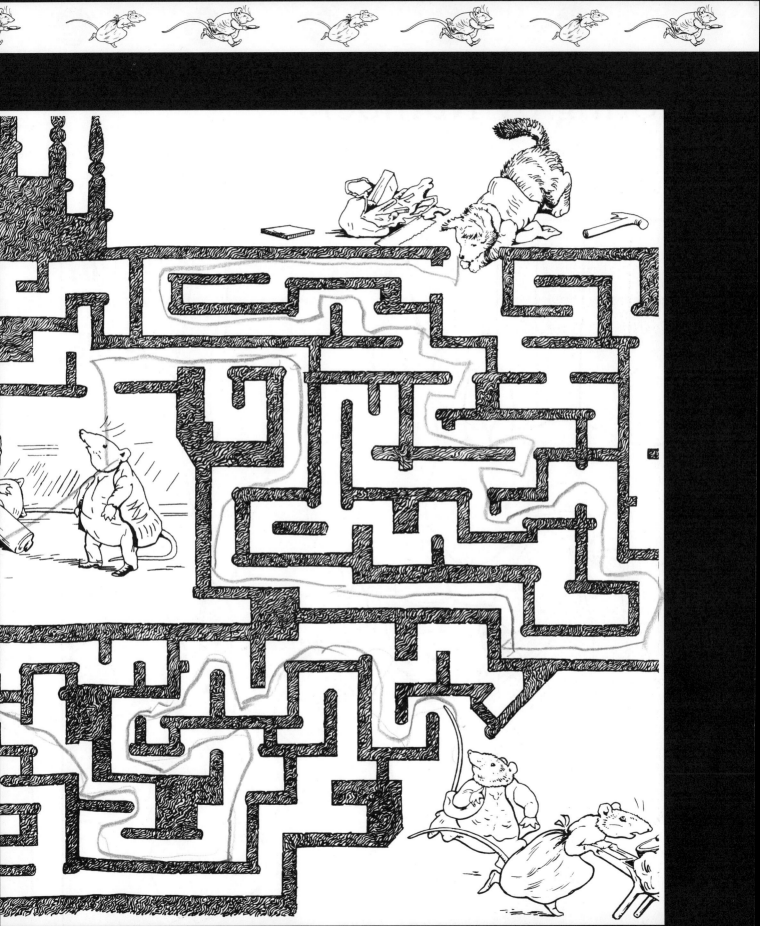

Coloring by Numbers

Mrs. Rabbit is sending the rabbits down the lane to gather blackberries. Color the picture, looking at the letters and using the key above to choose your colors.

Shadow Puzzle

Can you guess which of Peter Rabbit's friends these shadows belong to?
Write their names on the line below each one.

1. _____

2. _____

3. _____

4. _____

5. _____

Spot the Difference

See if you can spot six differences between these two pictures from *The Tale of Benjamin Bunny*. When you have finished, color them in.

Mrs. Tiggy-Winkle's Word Square

Can you circle twenty words from *The Tale of Mrs. Tiggy-Winkle* in this word square? The words may be found going up, down, forward, backward and diagonally. To help you the words are listed below.

R	M	H	Y	T	E	K	C	A	J	P	Z	E	W	Q
H	A	I	R	P	I	N	S	K	S	A	L	M	A	U
G	W	A	I	S	T	C	O	A	T	I	N	H	S	A
B	O	R	F	E	L	A	L	K	G	S	L	C	H	H
M	S	A	J	E	K	H	M	O	E	V	B	R	I	T
I	E	L	R	I	I	A	R	V	T	E	K	A	N	O
T	H	E	D	G	E	H	O	G	S	H	I	T	G	L
T	T	R	L	N	I	L	C	B	R	S	E	S	J	C
E	A	A	M	U	G	K	G	R	U	V	N	S	C	E
N	H	S	I	R	C	B	A	T	E	N	U	M	V	L
S	H	A	W	L	P	I	E	P	A	K	D	T	R	B
A	P	R	I	C	K	L	E	S	B	I	D	L	B	A
T	M	G	E	O	N	G	C	R	G	R	U	N	E	T
H	Y	A	E	S	S	V	E	R	N	O	R	P	A	S
A	R	D	E	B	A	S	K	E	T	N	B	A	N	H

IRON
LUCIE
HANDKERCHIEF
HEDGEHOG
APRON
PRICKLES
TABLECLOTH
GLOVES
MITTENS
STARCH
CLOTHES
JACKET
WASHING
BASKET
WAISTCOAT
TEA
HAIRPINS
BUNDLES
SHAWL
PEGS

Mr. Jeremy Fisher's Crossword

Answer the clues across and down to fill in the words in the crossword. All the words can be found in Beatrix Potter's story *The Tale of Mr. Jeremy Fisher*.

Across

2 A black water creature that tweaks Mr. Jeremy's toe (11)

5 A prickly fish called Jack Sharp! (11)

7 Mr. Jeremy wears these to stop his feet getting wet (8)

8 A green waterproof jacket (9)

10 Mr. Jeremy uses one of these as a boat (8)

Down

1 Little fish that Mr. Jeremy tries to catch for dinner (7)

3 Water that falls from the sky (4)

4 Great big fish that pulls Mr. Jeremy underwater (5)

6 Bait used to catch fish (5)

9 A slimy creature that lives in a shell (5)

Puzzle Pieces

Tom Thumb and Hunca Munca are being very bad mice and smashing up the plates in the doll's house. The six puzzle pieces below all fit somewhere in the picture. Color the picture in and then see if you can find where the six puzzle pieces come from.

Counting Fun

The Tailor of Gloucester is busy in his workshop making clothes. He has lots of mouse helpers. How many mice can you see in the picture? When you have counted them, color it in.

Answers

Character Links

Jemima Puddle-Duck - **duckling**
Benjamin Bunny - **onions**
Peter Rabbit - **watering can**
Tom Kitten - **buttons**
Mrs. Tiggy-Winkle - **iron**
Mr. Jeremy Fisher - **fish**

Squirrel Nutkin's Riddles

Ninny Nanny Netticoat - **a candle**
Hitty Pitty - **a nettle**
Riddle me, Riddle me, Rot-tot-tote! - **a red cherry**

Shadow Puzzle

1. Benjamin Bunny
2. Squirrel Nutkin
3. Mrs. Tittlemouse
4. Jemima Puddle-Duck
5. Tom Kitten

Spot the Difference

Mrs. Tiggy-Winkle's Word Square

Mr. Jeremy Fisher's Crossword

Across
2. Waterbeetle
5. Stickleback
7. Goloshes
8. Macintosh
10. Lilyleaf

Down
1. Minnows
3. Rain
4. Trout
6. Worms
9. Snail

Puzzle Pieces

Counting Fun

There are 15 mice in the picture.